D1295379

The Adventures of
BOFFEE BEARS

CLB 3533
Published by Binky Books
An imprint of Grange Books PLC
The Grange
Grange Yard
London SE1 3AG
This edition published 1994

ISBN 1 85627 473 X
Printed and bound in Spain by Graficas Estella

STORY BY STEPHEN ATTMORE
ILLUSTRATED BY ANGELA MILLS

CONTENTS

Who are the BOFFEE Bears?

Have you ever wondered what happens to teddy bears when children no longer care for them?

What do they get up to? Where do they go?

This is the story of three of them. There is BB, their leader, who keeps them in order and is always full of clever ideas; Tatty Ted endears himself to reader and listener alike with his cheeky humour and bumbling antics, and Ragtime is a musical bear with a song for every occasion. Find out more about the BOFFEE Bears by reading this story.

MEET THE
BOFFEE BEARS

There is a special place where teddy bears go when they are left on their own with nobody to look after them. Not many people know about this place. Let us take a look.

There is a little lane leading to a quiet little cottage. The name on the gate is "Windy House". Funny name for a cottage!

Can you see the bear walking along the lane? The bear is carrying a large bag. It is nearly dragging on the ground. What a heavy thing for a bear to bear!

What a nice day to be out for a walk. The sun is shining – shine, shine – the birds are singing – sing, sing – and the little bulbs are peeping out – peep, peep!

Something comes hurtling down the slope. What is it? Is it a bird? Don't be silly! Birds fly, they don't roll down hills. It could be a train.

"Whooooooooooooooooooaaaaaaaaaaaaaaa!"

That's a funny noise for a train to make. The thing is heading straight for the bear with the heavy bag. Look out! Too late. The fast moving blob hits the slow moving bear like a runaway wheel hitting a skittle.

Bump! Crash! Up in the air goes the bear and her bag. Thump! Ouch! Down comes the bear on top of the – er – thing.

The bear is angry and annoyed. Clumsy ... mutter, mutter ... should look where it's going ... grrr!"

The bear stops and looks at the lump on the ground. "What shall I do with this?"

The bear is about to give the heap a friendly kick when a little squeak comes from somewhere. The bear bends down to listen.

“Hello, mate”, says a tiny voice.

Amazing! The furry lump speaks! What is more amazing, the furry lump moves. The lump shakes itself and dust flies everywhere.

“You could say hello back,” says the dusty bear. “Do you always stand around with your mouth open? You want to be careful, you might swallow something nasty!”

The first bear stares at the scruffy urchin.

“Ted E. Bear at your service,” says the dusty bear.

“You look more like Tatty Bear,” mutters the other bear.

“Tatty Bear. I like that! Yeh, you can call me Tatty Ted. What’s your name?”

The smart bear replies, “My name is BB.”

Ted starts laughing. “BeeBee! What sort of a name is that?

BeeBee. You don’t sting, do you? Hee, hee!”

He laughs so much he nearly splits his sides.

BB scowls. “BB means baby. Once upon a time I was loved like a baby. I’m very proud of my name.”

BB turns to go. “Hey, wait for me!” shouts Ted. “Where are we going?”

“I am off to the library to change my books.”

“What into? Frogs?” jokes Ted. “Are you going to change them into frogs?” He falls over again, laughing at his own joke.

“Do you always fall over?” asks BB.

“Oh yes, always. I fell last night as well.”

“Sorry to hear that,” says BB.

“Oh, I enjoyed it,” chirps Ted. “I fell asleep. Ha, ha!”

He is a funny little bear. BB can’t help feeling sorry for him. He needs someone to look after him. “Keep up with me. Right, left, right, left!” BB shouts, as she marches down the lane.

“Right, left, right, left?” Tatty Ted turns right, then left, then right again and then … falls over again. He stands up and then sits down. He feels all dizzy!

Where is BB? Poor Tatty Ted. What will he do now?

After a few minutes, Ted remembers that BB said something about going to the library. Where is that? He has no idea.

There is a large caravan up ahead. He goes inside. "Excuse me!" he shouts. Silence. "Is this a library?"

"Shhhhhhhhhh!"

"Who said that?" asks Ted. A lady libearian pops her head round a huge pile of books. "Shhhhhhhhh!" she repeats, pointing to a large notice hanging from the roof.

Ted starts to explain that he is not too good with these letter thingies that they have on signs …

"Shhhhhhhhhhh!"

The lady libearian comes right up to Tatty Ted and looks at him over the top of her glasses. "Oooh! she looks fierce," thinks Ted.

"My name is Ted. Full name Edward Eustace Bear, but you can call me Tatty Ted. What's your name?"

"Shhhhhhhhhhhh!"

"That's a funny name!"

Tatty Ted spies his new friend. “There you are, BB! Bet you can’t guess the name of that old battleaxe with the glasses!”

“Shhhhhhhhh!”

“How did you know?”

“Now listen, Mr Bear,” whispers BB, “shut up and behave or you will get us thrown out.”

Tatty Ted takes the hint. He starts to sulk. He looks at all the books. There is one on the top shelf with a pretty picture on the cover. Ted reaches up. No good. He stands on tiptoe. Still no good. He climbs onto the bottom shelf. He stretches up – got it. Aaaaaargh! Ted falls backward, pulling lots and lots and lots of books down with him. The libearian is very angry. Look out, Ted!

Library

"We must get home before you get yourself into any more trouble!" says BB.

"Whatever you say, boss!" Ted salutes and pokes himself in the eye. "Now I know what BB is for – Bossy Boots. Hee, hee!"

BB marches off down the lane at a fast pace. Ted stumbles along behind as fast as his little legs will carry him. Then the two bears stop. They stand and listen. This is what they hear.

"If you go down the lane today,
You'll get a big surprise,
For you will meet a tatty bear,
With patches and brown eyes."

"When you're on the way home today,
There's an even bigger surprise,
To find the singer don't look round,
Look up, yes, to the skies."

The singing bear tells them that his name is Ragtime. BB invites Ragtime to come and stay at "Windy House."

That evening, as the three sit in front of the fire, Ragtime tells the other two that he was sitting in the tree while his clothes were drying. He had once belonged to a sailor who sailed the seven seas, and one day the ship was hit by a whale.

"You should have taken your clothes off and hung them over the branch," BB says – always full of bright ideas.

"Then he would be a bare bear," adds Ted cheekily. "Or an 'I don't care' bear! Hee, hee!"

Ragtime changes the subject. "How about forming a troupe?" he suggests. "We could call ourselves the Three Bears."

"BOFFEE Bears," says BB. "BOFFEE for Best of Friends For Ever and Ever." So that was decided upon.

Meet the BOFFEE Bears – BB, Ragtime and Tatty Ted.

BOFFEE BEARS'
SURPRISE

The three BOFFEE Bears are resting before they start on the long trek home. BB has her nose in a book called "Tales of the Riverbank." Ragtime is strumming his banjo – as usual. Tatty Ted is skimming stones across the top of the water.

"How about this one then?" continues Ted. "How do you start a teddy bear race?"

"Don't know," says a voice from somewhere. "How do you start a teddy bear race?"

"Say 'Ready, teddy, go'!" shouts Tatty Ted.

"Ha, ha, ha! That's a good one."

"Thank you," says Ted. "And there's more ..."

"That's enough," says BB. "I'm trying to read."

"But I thought you liked my jokes," groans Ted. "You were laughing at them."

"No, I was not," say BB and Ragtime together.

"Well, some bear was," mutters Ted. He looks round. There is no other bear to be seen. Tatty Ted decides to try another joke. Then he can find out who is laughing. "Who is related?"

There is no answer. "You don't know?" says Ted. "Then I'll tell you, It's me running in a relay race. Relay Ted."

Ha, ha, ha! Giggle, giggle.

"There," says Tatty Ted, "one of you was laughing!"

"It was not me!" say BB and Ragtime together.

The three BOFFEE Bears look around. Where is the laughing and giggling coming from?

Tatty Ted points to the brick wall. The three bears walk across and peep over the wall. What do you think they see there?

"What are you doing here, Fran?" asks BB.

"She should be at the orphanage," says Ragtime.

"No!" shrieks Fran. "I don't want to go back there. I want to stay with you. I want to be a BOFFEE Bear."

Ted looks at Ragtime. Ragtime looks at BB. BB looks at Tatty Ted. Tatty Ted looks ... scruffy!

"Don't be too hard on her," says Ted.

"We think you should go back to the orphanage, Fran," says BB. "You're not old enough to be a BOFFEE Bear."

"But I don't know where it is!" cries Fran. "I've been following you all morning. I don't know where to go!" Here come the tears. "Whaaaa!"

Ragtime fetches his banjo. He sings a soothing song.

"There, there, listen to me,
The BOFFEE Bears are here –
Ragtime, Ted and BB –
We'll bring you lots of cheer."

Tatty Ted and BB join in on the second verse – which is the same as the first. Fran joins in with the third verse – which is the same as the first verse and the second verse.

BB lifts Fran onto the wall. From there she jumps onto Ted's back. They set off to find the orphanage.

"It's this way!" shouts Fran. "No, it's not. It's that way."

This happens several times. The bears walk this way, that way, every way. The sun is getting tired. It is going to its bed. It will be dark soon. Will they ever find the orphanage?

It is dark now. The sun has gone to bed. Tatty Ted keeps bumping into things. Fran is crying. She is scared.

"What do you call a lost teddy?" says Tatty Ted.

"Don't know," replies Fran.

"Teddy where," says Tatty Ted. No bear laughs.

BB orders the bears to stand back to back. "Look ahead of you and tell me if you can see any lights."

After a short pause, Ragtime shouts, "There!"

Where? Over there. Yes, there are some lights on in a house. The four bears set off once more heading towards the lights.

As they get closer, Fran skips along, flapping her arms. This is it. This is the orphanage. It is a large building.

Ragtime picks Fran up so that the little bear can knock on the door.

Knock. Knock. Knock. Knock. Knock. Knock!
"That's enough!"

The lady bear who looks after all the orphan bears opens the door. She is so pleased to see Fran.

"These are the BOFFEE Bears," says Fran proudly.

The lady bear asks the BOFFEE Bears to come in. She shakes each of them by the paw.

"How many little bears do you have here, Ms...?" asks BB.

"Mrs Foster," answers the lady bear. "Over forty bears now."

She invites the BOFFEE Bears to stay the night. They are very grateful. It is no fun wandering around in the dark.

Soon they are seated with Fran at a large table with a large supper spread out in front of them. While they are eating, Mrs Foster tells them that many of the bears in the orphanage come there when their owners don't want them any more. They find new homes for some of them, but many end up staying there for the rest of their days.

In the morning, Fran is very upset. Her friends the BOFFEE Bears are leaving. She begs Tatty Ted to tell her and some friends a knock-knock joke. Then they want to hear another – and another. BB says it is time they were going. So Ted tells one final joke.

"Knock, knock!"

"Who's there?" chorus the bears.

"Les," says Ted.

"Les who?" ask the bears.

"Les stop telling knock-knock jokes."

Fran and her friends ask Ragtime to sing them a song. Ragtime sings "We're leaving home, bye bye ..." The little bears burst into tears. Mrs Foster whispers something in BB's ear. Then the three bears set off.

On the way home, BB explains to Ragtime and Tatty Ted what Mrs Foster said to her as they left the orphanage.

It is not a secret really. The BOFFEE Bears call back at the orphanage a few weeks later. It is Christmas Day. They are helping at the bears' party. BB has put herself in charge of party games. She is having trouble keeping some of the bears in order!

"Don't do that, George!" she shouts at one of the bears, who is trying to pin the donkey's tail onto Fran.

Ragtime is in a corner. Some of the orphan bears around him are singing carols, such as "We Three Bears of Orient Are" and "The Little Drummer Bear." Tatty Ted is giving bearback rides. He is nearly out of breath. The little bears are having a great time!

Here comes Christmas Bear! He has a present for everyone.

"Three cheers for the BOFFEE Bears!" shouts little Fran.

"Hip, hip ... hooray!"

BOFFEE BEAR'S
BIRTHDAY

"Hip hip hooray! It's my birthday!" shouts Tatty Ted. He jumps up and down on his bed. Ouch! He forgets he is in the bottom bunk.

Tatty Ted has an amazing memory. He can only remember one thing – his own birthday! He tells every bear he meets when his birthday is and what presents he would like.

Ted is not sure how old he is. He knows he has been around for a long time because once he heard someone say, "What, that old thing! That's been around for years!"

He is happy because it is his birthday. "Happy birthday to me, happy birthday to me." He jumps into his trousers, then he jumps into his jumper and then he jumps into the air!

Tatty Ted rushes out of the bedroom. There are so many exciting things to do. He charges along, trips and rolls head over heels until he hits the front door. As he sits up, some envelopes pop through the letterbox and drop onto his head.

Oh, he is so excited! Which ones are for him? He is not sure. The names are not easy to read. They must be for him – it is his birthday. He paws open the first one. “That’s not a birthday card! That must be for Bill!”

“You’re up early,” says a sleepy Ragtime. “It must be a special day. Don’t tell me. It’s someone’s birthday.”

“He knows,” thinks Ted.

“No,” says Ragtime, “it’s St Edward’s Day and you are going to bring me breakfast in bed. Remember, I’m in the top bunk.”

"What about these?" shouts Tatty Ted. Ragtime sorts the envelopes. There are three for BB, three for Ragtime, two for Bill, seven for the bear who used to live in Windy House and ...

"None for you today, Ted. Never mind, you get on with that breakfast. And hurry. I'm starving," says Ragtime.

Perhaps the postbear forgot to leave Ted's cards. Or maybe BB and Ragtime have hidden them. Yes, that's it. Hunt the cards. Now where are they? Ted rushes here, there, everywhere and back to here. They must be somewhere. And what about all the presents? They should be easy to find because they are big! He only asked for big things. No, they are not there. Or there. Or there.

Tatty Ted is slowing down now. He looks very unhappy.

"Good morning," says BB, looking bright and cheerful. "What's good about it?" grumbles Ted, shuffling his feet even more than usual.

There is a knock at the door. Knock, knock! Sorry, there are two knocks at the door.

"Who's there?" shouts BB.

"Harry," comes the reply.

"Harry who?" says BB.

"Harry up and open this door!"

BB opens the front door. Standing there is one of BB's cousins – Digby. He is holding out an empty pot.

"Oh, is that for me?" says Ted. It must be a present.

"No, it ain't!" says Digby, rolling the pot to his tummy.

"Oi've come for a refill. I want some more of that there luv'ly, sticky, gooey stuff called honey. Yum, yum!"

BB invites Digby in for breakfast. BB asks him what he would like to eat.

"Oi'll eat anything with honey in," says Digby. He tells BB that when he was a young bear he didn't like eating. Then one day he had honey on a piece of bread. That was lovely. Now he only eats things with honey in them or on them.

Ragtime has given up waiting for his breakfast to be brought to him. He wanders into the room and says to Tatty Ted, "You look like a bear with a sore head. You're not ill, are you?"

"E moight have a touch of bearybeary!" says Digby, his mouth full of honey cake. He starts to laugh and a spray of crumbs shoots out of his mouth. They splatter Ted from head to waist. Ted stomps out of the room.

Ted E Bear walks round and round the yard. He tries counting to ten. "One, two, three ... ten."

"Good morning," says a voice from the other side of the hedge. "Pray tell me where I might find the BOFFEE Bears?"

"Right here," says Tatty Ted, cheering up a little.

The gate opens and ... look who it is! Ted says, "Hello, Mr J. Have you called to wish me a happy birthday?"

Mr J walks straight past Ted. "No," he says. "I was just passing and thought I would look in on BB. She makes a super cup of tea, you know. In the cottage, is she?"

That does it! Tatty Ted is really, really, really unhappy now. They have all forgotten his birthday. He shuffles back into the cottage. He goes up to the attic. He mopes, he sulks, he kicks an old trunk. Ouch!

Ted slumps down on his bed. He buries his face in the pillow. What a miserable birthday he is having! He sobs and sobs. They are big, heaving sobs. In fact, he sobs so much that he cries himself to sleep.

Tatty Ted dreams a strange dream. In this dream he swallows a worm. "Quick, drink some water!" says a dream bear. "No," replies Ted. "I'm too angry. Let him walk." All the bears laugh. Are they laughing at him? A bear at the back of the crowd calls out, "Edward!" Who is that? "Ted!"

Ted sits up in bed. That is Ragtime calling him.

"I must have fallen asleep," says Ted.

He falls out of bed and slouches out into the garden.

"HAPPY BIRTHDAY, TED!"

Ted stands and stares. Wow! What an amazing sight! More presents than you can imagine and a cake so big it would make a bear's eyes pop out of his head if he ate it all. Ted doesn't know what to say. Where did they hide all those presents?

Ragtime sings, "This is a surprise ..."
The other bears join in "Oh yes it is."
"For your birthday – oh yes it is,
We love you Teddy – oh yes we do,
Even your jokes – oh yes we do."

Ted gets stuck in.

"That's the fourth honey cake you've had," says Mr J. "Everyone who sees you going back time and time again will think you're a pig!"

"They won't," replies Ted. "I'll tell them it's for you!"

A BOFFEE BEAR
ON THE MOON

The BOFFEE Bears are three happy, well-fed bears. It was a good idea to have a night-time bearbecue! Which clever bear thought of doing this? It was BB – the Brainy Bear. She asks Ragtime and Ted if they would like any more food.

"No thank you," says Ragtime politely.

"Not for me," says Ted. "I'm full up!"

Ragtime looks up at the sky. He says, "What would you do, Ted, if a spaceship landed here and little green people came out of it?"

"I don't know," answers Tatty Ted. "But I can tell what I *wouldn't* do."

"What's that?"

"I wouldn't wait around for them to get ripe!"

BB starts to tell the other two about her friend Jake who's got a wooden leg.

Ted says, "That nothing. My mate's got a wooden chest!"

BB explains that Jake was a one-eyed panda whose leg was pulled so often that it came off one day. They took him to the toy hospital and he had a wooden leg fitted.

Then Tatty Ted tells of when he went to the toy hospital.

"I says to the doctor, 'Doctor, I'm worried. I keep hearing voices but I don't see anyone.'

'When does it happen?' says Doctor Fixit.

'Every time I answer the phone,' I says. Hee, hee!"

The BOFFEE Bears have not laughed so much in a long time. Have you ever seen bears laughing? They rock back and forth, roll from side to side, then fall back and wave their legs in the air.

Tatty Ted looks up at the Moon. It is smiling down at him. Is that a bear sitting on the Moon? No, he must be seeing things!

"Is there such a thing as a Moonbear?" asks Ted.

"Don't believe those old stories," says Ragtime."

"There is something up there," Ted says, going cross-eyed.

BB starts telling another story about her friend Jake.

About the time he turned up at the teddy bears' picnic with a toy parrot on his shoulder. Jake spent the afternoon feeding seedcake to the toy parrot and trying to teach it to say "pieces of eight!"

Tatty Ted tries to laugh but as soon as he opens his mouth a big yawn comes out.

"I'm not boring you, am I?" asks BB.

"No, of course not!" replies Tatty Ted.

"Did I tell you about the time I went to a fancy dress party dressed as a bookworm?" says BB.

"A what?" asks Ted.

"A bookworm," replies BB. "I was wearing my glasses and carrying a large book. I had a strange costume made from ..."

Ragtime picks up his banjo and starts singing,

"Come fly, come fly with me ...
and I will take you to the moon ..."

"Now that is an idea," thinks Tatty Ted. It is so warm in front of the fire that he begins to feel sleepy. Ted *f a a alls* asleep. He dreams he is flying to the moon. Up, up and away!

Is Tatty Ted really going to the Moon?

Wheeeeee! This is great fun! Tatty Ted turns over and floats on his back. Then he tries a somersault. Then he loops the loop. Show off!

Ted can see tiny figures down below. There are BB and Ragtime sitting beside the fire. Who is that with them? "It looks like me," thinks Ted. "Can't be! I'm up here."

Down on the ground, Ragtime finishes the song. BB begins another of her stories. She will go on for hours, if you let her. This story is about when she was a young bear.

"I thought she'd always been old!" says Ted.

"Did you say something, Ted?" asks BB.

The sleeping mound on the ground does not answer. "That was a lucky escape!" thinks Ted. "I must remember not to talk in my sleep. Well, I've got work to do. I must see if there is a Moonbear!"

"As I was saying," says BB to Ragtime. "Those kids played with their space toys and computers morning, noon and night. They didn't play with me. But I'll tell you something. You can't cuddle those space toys, but you can cuddle me."

"Oh, is that an offer?" says Ragtime.

"Not you!" shouts BB. "Keep your paws to yourself! I meant those dear children. I was so lonely. There was nothing else to do but read. I read and re-read every book in that room."

"SNORE!"

"That is typical of you, Edward Eustace Bear," says BB." We listen to all your so-called funny stories, but when I talk about something important, you fall asleep. Charming!"

Although he is asleep, Tatty Ted can hear what BB is saying. He knows what it is like to be unwanted and unloved. He knows about those space toys ... zap! zap!

"You must understand," says BB to Ragtime, "that I didn't mind being zapped with space guns. What upset me was the time they spent on the computer. Hours and hours they spent clicking away on that ... what's it called? Erm ... mouse."

"Mouse?" says Ragtime.

"Yes, a mouse. They plug it into a computer by its tail and then chase it round the table."

"Poor mouse!" groans Ragtime. "You should start a protest group. Call it SCAM – Stop Cruelty to All Mice!"

BB is trying not to cry. Why does she always cry when she recalls her past? Is it because she was so lonely then?

Some of these things seep through to the bear brain inside sleeping Ted's head. Zap ... mouse ... tail ... SCAM! Poor old BB! ... unloved ... fancy being second choice to a mouse thingy!

Ragtime starts singing "Somewhere over the Moonbeam."

"Moonbeam," thinks Ted. "That is what I must do – find a moonbeam. Who knows where I can find a moonbeam? I bet the Moonbear does." Ted turns towards the moon. Must go faster. Why can't I go faster? Are you there, Moonbear?"

He thinks he can see the Moonbear. Yes, there it is. No, it's gone again. Ted shouts at the top of his voice, "Help!" His voice echoes across the sky.

There is the Moonbear again. "Please help me find a moonbeam." The Moonbear says nothing. It looks so sad.

"WAKE UP! Wake up!" BB shakes Tatty Ted. "Wake up, Ted. You were shouting," says BB, "Are you all right?"

Slowly Ted sits up and looks around him. "We love you, BB," he says. Then he gives BB a big bearhug.

BOFFEE BEARS
ON HOLIDAY

The BOFFEE Bears are going on holiday. They are not sure where they are going or how they will get there. You see, it all started like this ...

A few hours ago – well, yesterday evening actually – Tatty Ted was eating bearbecue food. Ragtime the musical bear was singing a song about eating! BB was staring into space, thinking.

Suddenly BB jumps up and yells "I've got it!"

Ragtime thinks that BB has gone hopping mad. "Call me an ambulance," he says to Ted.

"All right," says Ted. "You're an ambulance!"

"I have had a brainwave," shouts BB. "What we need is adventure. Something exciting. I know. Let us hit the road!"

BB starts packing all the things they will need – and a few extras as well. "Early to bed, early to rise," says BB.

"Up at the crack of dawn, fellow bears."

A few hours later, Tatty Ted is having a sweet dream. He is at a bears' picnic and all the food is for him.

Then something shakes him. Help! What is it?

"Shake a leg, you lazy bear!" shouts BB. "It's time we were on the move."

"But I haven't heard the crack of dawn yet," moans Ted.

The sun is up. BB is standing beside the cases. She is fur-ious.

"Where are those two lazy bears? Why can I never get help when I need it?" she moans.

Tatty Ted and Ragtime walk hand in hand. "Now come along, you two!" snaps BB. "Help me load these things!"

Ted and Ragtime know when not to argue with BB. So in the time it takes to count to forty-three, they load all the cases and boxes.

Now BB is studying a map and Ragtime is strumming his banjo. He sings something about going on a summer holiday. Where is Tatty Ted? He is in the caravan, making a start on the lunch!

Ragtime whispers in BB's ear, "Haven't you forgotten something?"

"Don't think so," says BB. "I packed everything we need."

"Then can you tell me why we are not moving?" says Ragtime. "This may be because there is nothing pulling us!"

BB puts her head in her paws. Oh dear! What can they do?

Think. Think. Think harder. Come on BB. You can do it.

Knock, knock!

"Who's there?" asks Ragtime.

"Fur," says a voice inside the caravan.

"Fur who?" Ragtime asks.

"Fur goodness sake, let me out!" squeaks Tatty Ted.

At last BB has the answer. Look who is between the shafts! Will the BOFFEE Bears ever get away on their holiday?

"Four wheels on our caravan
But we're not moving along ..."

Tatty Ted is not amused by Ragtime's song. He is lying in a heap on the ground. The bears have not moved at all. What a holiday!

But who is this striding along the lane? "Good day to you," says the new bear. "I see that you are also travellers on the highway of life. I am known to my friends as Mr J."

BB asks Mr J, "Do you know how to move a caravan?"

Mr J suggests that two of them should pull together. What a good idea! Ragtime joins Tatty Ted in the shafts and Mr J joins BB inside for a cup of tea and a slice of honey loaf.

Mr J tells BB his life story. He was a well-to-do bear with pots of honey. When the family he lodged with moved to another country they could not take Mr J with them. It was too dangerous. Bears can catch things like bearfoot rot and rabies.

"Oh how awful!" exclaims BB, raising her paws in the air.

Tatty Ted pops his head through the window. "I know about rabbits," he says. "Soft, fluffy things with big ears."

"Not rabbits, straw brain!" shouts BB. "Rabies! Get back to pulling the caravan! By the way, where are we?"

"In the same place," grumbles a ragged looking Ragtime.

Mr J suggests they all get behind the caravan and push together. "One, two, three ... heave!" shouts Mr J. The bears fall flat on their faces. They look up to see their home rolling slowly down the lane away from them.

"Edward Eustace Bear, if you don't stop that runaway home you won't get any supper!" shouts BB.

Tatty Ted is off. He is weaving about all over the place. Ragtime can feel a song coming on. Where is his banjo? It is on the caravan. "Ted!" he calls out. "Grab my banjo!"

The rollaway home bumps into a stone. Ted tries to grab the banjo as it flies through the air. He falls over and rolls head over heels. He rolls past the caravan, off the track and straight into a pond. Splash!

"Hey! You can't swim here!" shouts Ragtime.

"Glug, glug! I'm not swimming," comes the soggy reply. "I'm stopping myself from sinking."

Tatty Ted is clutching Ragtime's banjo in his damp paw.

The BOFFEE bears decide to leave the caravan where it is. BB is trying to light a fire so that Tatty Ted can dry his clothes. "This match won't light!" she cries.

"That's funny," says Ted. "It did this morning."

Mr J picks up his stick and tells the others that it is time he was on his way.

"May I be so bold," says BB, "as to ask where a bear of the road like yourself is heading?"

"I am off to seek fame and fortune," says Mr J proudly.

Tatty Ted asks Mr J if he knows where fame and fortune live.

As they wave goodbye to Mr J, Ragtime starts to sing.

"We were going on a summer holiday,
No more effort for a week or two.
But it's hard work to get under way,
A lot of effort for me and you.

Now we're taking our summer holiday,
Beside the lane – it's a quiet spot.
We wish you were here with us today,
Ted got wet but the sun was hot."